A COLLECTION OF KATE CHOPIN'S SHORT STORIES
BY

Kate Chopin

Beyond the Bayou

The bayou curved like a crescent around the point of land on which La Folle's cabin stood. Between the stream and the hut lay a big abandoned field, where cattle were pastured when the bayou supplied them with water enough. Through the woods that spread back into unknown regions the woman had drawn an imaginary line, and past this circle she never stepped. This was the form of her only mania.

She was now a large, gaunt black woman, past thirty-five. Her real name was Jacqueline, but every one on the plantation called her La Folle, because in childhood she had been frightened literally "out of her senses," and had never wholly regained them.

It was when there had been skirmishing and sharpshooting all day in the woods. Evening was near when P'tit Maitre, black with powder and crimson with blood, had staggered into the cabin of Jacqueline's mother, his pursuers close at his heels. The sight had stunned her childish reason.

She dwelt alone in her solitary cabin, for the rest of the quarters had long since been removed beyond her sight and knowledge. She had more physical strength than most men, and made her patch of cotton and corn and tobacco like the best of them. But of the world beyond the bayou she had long known nothing, save what her morbid fancy conceived.

People at Bellissime had grown used to her and her way, and they thought nothing of it. Even when "Old Mis'" died, they did not wonder that La Folle had not crossed the bayou, but had stood upon her side of it, wailing and lamenting.

P'tit Maitre was now the owner of Bellissime. He was a middle-aged man, with a family of beautiful daughters about him, and a little son whom La Folle loved as if he had been her own. She called him Cheri, and so did every one else because she did.

None of the girls had ever been to her what Cheri was. They had each and all loved to be with her, and to listen to her wondrous stories of things that always happened "yonda, beyon' de bayou."

But none of them had stroked her black hand quite as Cheri did, nor rested their heads against her knee so confidingly, nor fallen asleep in her arms as he used to do. For Cheri hardly did such things now, since he had become the proud possessor of a gun, and had had his black curls cut off.

That summer—the summer Cheri gave La Folle two black curls tied with a knot of red ribbon—the water ran so low in the bayou that even the little children at Bellissime were able to cross it on foot, and the cattle were sent to pasture down by the river. La Folle was sorry when they were gone, for she loved these dumb companions well, and liked to feel that they were there, and to hear them browsing by night up to her own enclosure.

It was Saturday afternoon, when the fields were deserted. The men had flocked to a neighboring village to do their week's trading, and the women were occupied with household affairs,—La Folle as well as the others. It was then she mended and washed her handful of clothes, scoured her house, and did her baking.

In this last employment she never forgot Cheri. To-day she had fashioned croquignoles of the most fantastic and alluring shapes for him. So when she saw the boy come trudging across the old field with his gleaming little new rifle on his shoulder, she called out gayly to him, "Cheri! Cheri!"

But Cheri did not need the summons, for he was coming straight to her. His pockets all bulged out with almonds and raisins and an orange that he had secured for her from the very fine dinner which had been given that day up at his father's house.

He was a sunny-faced youngster of ten. When he had emptied his pockets, La Folle patted his round red cheek, wiped his soiled hands on her apron, and smoothed his hair. Then she watched him as, with his cakes in his hand, he crossed her strip of cotton back of the cabin, and disappeared into the wood.

He had boasted of the things he was going to do with his gun out there.

"You think they got plenty deer in the wood, La Folle?" he had inquired, with the calculating air of an experienced hunter.

"Non, non!" the woman laughed. "Don't you look fo' no deer, Cheri. Dat's too big. But you bring La Folle one good fat squirrel fo' her dinner to-morrow, an' she goin' be satisfi'."

"One squirrel ain't a bite. I'll bring you mo' 'an one, La Folle," he had boasted pompously as he went away.

When the woman, an hour later, heard the report of the boy's rifle close to the wood's edge, she would have thought nothing of it if a sharp cry of distress had not followed the sound.

She withdrew her arms from the tub of suds in which they had been plunged, dried them upon her apron, and as quickly as her trembling limbs would bear her, hurried to the spot whence the ominous report had come.

It was as she feared. There she found Cheri stretched upon the ground, with his rifle beside him. He moaned piteously:—

"I'm dead, La Folle! I'm dead! I'm gone!"

"Non, non!" she exclaimed resolutely, as she knelt beside him. "Put you' arm 'roun' La Folle's nake, Cheri. Dat's nuttin'; dat goin' be nuttin'." She lifted him in her powerful arms.

Cheri had carried his gun muzzle-downward. He had stumbled,—he did not know how. He only knew that he had a ball lodged somewhere in his leg, and he thought that his end was at hand. Now, with his head upon the woman's shoulder, he moaned and wept with pain and fright.

"Oh, La Folle! La Folle! it hurt so bad! I can' stan' it, La Folle!"

"Don't cry, mon bebe, mon bebe, mon Cheri!" the woman spoke soothingly as she covered the ground with long strides. "La Folle goin' mine you; Doctor Bonfils goin' come make mon Cheri well agin."

She had reached the abandoned field. As she crossed it with her precious burden, she looked constantly and restlessly from side to side. A terrible fear was upon her,—the fear of the world beyond the bayou, the morbid and insane dread she had been under since childhood.

When she was at the bayou's edge she stood there, and shouted for help as if a life depended upon it:—

"Oh, P'tit Maitre! P'tit Maitre! Venez donc! Au secours! Au secours!"

No voice responded. Cheri's hot tears were scalding her neck. She called for each and every one upon the place, and still no answer came.

She shouted, she wailed; but whether her voice remained unheard or unheeded, no reply came to her frenzied cries. And all the while Cheri moaned and wept and entreated to be taken home to his mother.

La Folle gave a last despairing look around her. Extreme terror was upon her. She clasped the child close against her breast, where he could feel her heart beat like a muffled hammer. Then shutting her eyes, she ran suddenly down the shallow bank of the bayou, and never stopped till she had climbed the opposite shore.

She stood there quivering an instant as she opened her eyes. Then she plunged into the footpath through the trees.

She spoke no more to Cheri, but muttered constantly, "Bon Dieu, ayez pitie La Folle! Bon Dieu, ayez pitie moi!"

Instinct seemed to guide her. When the pathway spread clear and smooth enough before her, she again closed her eyes tightly against the sight of that unknown and terrifying world.

A child, playing in some weeds, caught sight of her as she neared the quarters. The little one uttered a cry of dismay.

"La Folle!" she screamed, in her piercing treble. "La Folle done cross de bayer!"

Quickly the cry passed down the line of cabins.

"Yonda, La Folle done cross de bayou!"

Children, old men, old women, young ones with infants in their arms, flocked to doors and windows to see this awe-inspiring spectacle. Most of them shuddered with superstitious dread of what it might portend. "She totin' Cheri!" some of them shouted.

Some of the more daring gathered about her, and followed at her heels, only to fall back with new terror when she turned her distorted face upon them. Her eyes were bloodshot and the saliva had gathered in a white foam on her black lips.

Some one had run ahead of her to where P'tit Maitre sat with his family and guests upon the gallery.

"P'tit Maitre! La Folle done cross de bayou! Look her! Look her yonda totin' Cheri!" This startling intimation was the first which they had of the woman's approach.

She was now near at hand. She walked with long strides. Her eyes were fixed desperately before her, and she breathed heavily, as a tired ox.

At the foot of the stairway, which she could not have mounted, she laid the boy in his father's arms. Then the world that had looked red to La Folle suddenly turned black,—like that day she had seen powder and blood.

She reeled for an instant. Before a sustaining arm could reach her, she fell heavily to the ground.

When La Folle regained consciousness, she was at home again, in her own cabin and upon her own bed. The moon rays, streaming in through the open door and windows, gave what light was needed to the old black mammy who stood at the table concocting a tisane of fragrant herbs. It was very late.

Others who had come, and found that the stupor clung to her, had gone again. P'tit Maitre had been there, and with him Doctor Bonfils, who said that La Folle might die.

But death had passed her by. The voice was very clear and steady with which she spoke to Tante Lizette, brewing her tisane there in a corner.

"Ef you will give me one good drink tisane, Tante Lizette, I b'lieve I'm goin' sleep, me."

And she did sleep; so soundly, so healthfully, that old Lizette without compunction stole softly away, to creep back through the moonlit fields to her own cabin in the new quarters.

The first touch of the cool gray morning awoke La Folle. She arose, calmly, as if no tempest had shaken and threatened her existence but yesterday.

She donned her new blue cottonade and white apron, for she remembered that this was Sunday. When she had made for herself a cup of strong black coffee, and drunk it with relish, she quitted the cabin and walked across the old familiar field to the bayou's edge again.

She did not stop there as she had always done before, but crossed with a long, steady stride as if she had done this all her life.

When she had made her way through the brush and scrub cottonwood-trees that lined the opposite bank, she found herself upon the border of a field where the white, bursting cotton, with the dew upon it, gleamed for acres and acres like frosted silver in the early dawn.

La Folle drew a long, deep breath as she gazed across the country. She walked slowly and uncertainly, like one who hardly knows how, looking about her as she went.

The cabins, that yesterday had sent a clamor of voices to pursue her, were quiet now. No one was yet astir at Bellissime. Only the birds that darted here and there from hedges were awake, and singing their matins.

When La Folle came to the broad stretch of velvety lawn that surrounded the house, she moved slowly and with delight over the springy turf, that was delicious beneath her tread.

She stopped to find whence came those perfumes that were assailing her senses with memories from a time far gone.

There they were, stealing up to her from the thousand blue violets that peeped out from green, luxuriant beds. There they were, showering down from the big waxen bells of the magnolias far above her head, and from the jessamine clumps around her.

There were roses, too, without number. To right and left palms spread in broad and graceful curves. It all looked like enchantment beneath the sparkling sheen of dew.

When La Folle had slowly and cautiously mounted the many steps that led up to the veranda, she turned to look back at the perilous ascent she had made. Then she caught sight of the river, bending like a silver bow at the foot of Bellissime. Exultation possessed her soul.

La Folle rapped softly upon a door near at hand. Cheri's mother soon cautiously opened it. Quickly and cleverly she dissembled the astonishment she felt at seeing La Folle.

"Ah, La Folle! Is it you, so early?"

"Oui, madame. I come ax how my po' li'le Cheri do, 's mo'nin'."

"He is feeling easier, thank you, La Folle. Dr. Bonfils says it will be nothing serious. He's sleeping now. Will you come back when he awakes?"

"Non, madame. I'm goin' wait yair tell Cheri wake up." La Folle seated herself upon the topmost step of the veranda.

A look of wonder and deep content crept into her face as she watched for the first time the sun rise upon the new, the beautiful world beyond the bayou.

MA'AME PELAGIE

I

When the war began, there stood on Cote Joyeuse an imposing mansion of red brick, shaped like the Pantheon. A grove of majestic live-oaks surrounded it.

Thirty years later, only the thick walls were standing, with the dull red brick showing here and there through a matted growth of clinging vines. The huge round pillars were intact; so to some extent was the stone flagging of hall and portico. There had been no home so stately along the whole stretch of Cote Joyeuse. Every one knew that, as they knew it had cost Philippe Valmet sixty thousand dollars to build, away back in 1840. No one was in danger of forgetting that fact, so long as his daughter Pelagie survived. She was a queenly, white-haired woman of fifty. "Ma'ame Pelagie," they called her, though she was unmarried, as was her sister Pauline, a child in Ma'ame Pelagie's eyes; a child of thirty-five.

The two lived alone in a three-roomed cabin, almost within the shadow of the ruin. They lived for a dream, for Ma'ame Pelagie's dream, which was to rebuild the old home.

It would be pitiful to tell how their days were spent to accomplish this end; how the dollars had been saved for thirty years and the picayunes hoarded; and yet, not half enough gathered! But Ma'ame Pelagie felt sure of twenty years of life before her, and counted upon as many more for her sister. And what could not come to pass in twenty—in forty—years?

Often, of pleasant afternoons, the two would drink their black coffee, seated upon the stone-flagged portico whose canopy was the blue sky of Louisiana. They loved to sit there in the silence, with only each other and the sheeny, prying lizards for company, talking of the old times and planning for the new; while light breezes stirred the tattered vines high up among the columns, where owls nested.

"We can never hope to have all just as it was, Pauline," Ma'ame Pelagie would say; "perhaps the marble pillars of the salon will have to be replaced by wooden ones, and the crystal candelabra left out. Should you be willing, Pauline?"

"Oh, yes Sesoeur, I shall be willing." It was always, "Yes, Sesoeur," or "No, Sesoeur," "Just as you please, Sesoeur," with poor little Mam'selle Pauline. For what did she remember of that old life and that old spendor? Only a faint gleam here and there; the half-consciousness of a young, uneventful existence; and then a great crash. That meant the nearness of war; the revolt of slaves; confusion ending in fire and flame through which she was borne safely in the strong arms of Pelagie, and carried to the log cabin which was still their home. Their brother, Leandre, had known more of it all than Pauline, and not so much as Pelagie. He had left the management of the big plantation with all its memories and traditions to his older sister, and had gone away to dwell in cities. That was many years ago. Now, Leandre's business called him frequently and upon long journeys from home, and his motherless daughter was coming to stay with her aunts at Cote Joyeuse.

They talked about it, sipping their coffee on the ruined portico. Mam'selle Pauline was terribly excited; the flush that throbbed into her pale, nervous face showed it; and she locked her thin fingers in and out incessantly.

"But what shall we do with La Petite, Sesoeur? Where shall we put her? How shall we amuse her? Ah, Seigneur!"

"She will sleep upon a cot in the room next to ours," responded Ma'ame Pelagie, "and live as we do. She knows how we live, and why we live; her father has told her. She knows we have money and could squander it if we chose. Do not fret, Pauline; let us hope La Petite is a true Valmet."

Then Ma'ame Pelagie rose with stately deliberation and went to saddle her horse, for she had yet to make her last daily round through the fields; and Mam'selle Pauline threaded her way slowly among the tangled grasses toward the cabin.

The coming of La Petite, bringing with her as she did the pungent atmosphere of an outside and dimly known world, was a shock to these two, living their dream-life. The girl was quite as tall as her aunt Pelagie, with dark eyes that reflected joy as a still pool reflects the light of stars; and her rounded cheek was tinged like the pink crepe myrtle. Mam'selle Pauline kissed her and trembled. Ma'ame Pelagie looked into her eyes with a searching gaze, which seemed to seek a likeness of the past in the living present.

And they made room between them for this young life.

II

La Petite had determined upon trying to fit herself to the strange, narrow existence which she knew awaited her at Cote Joyeuse. It went well enough at first. Sometimes she followed Ma'ame Pelagie into the fields to note how the cotton was opening, ripe and white; or to count the ears of corn upon the hardy stalks. But oftener she was with her aunt Pauline, assisting in household offices, chattering of her brief past, or walking with the older woman arm-in-arm under the trailing moss of the giant oaks.

Mam'selle Pauline's steps grew very buoyant that summer, and her eyes were sometimes as bright as a bird's, unless La Petite were away from her side, when they would lose all other light but one of uneasy expectancy. The girl seemed to love her well in return, and called her endearingly Tan'tante. But as the time went by, La Petite became very quiet,—not listless, but thoughtful, and slow in her movements. Then her cheeks began to pale, till they were tinged like the creamy plumes of the white crepe myrtle that grew in the ruin.

One day when she sat within its shadow, between her aunts, holding a hand of each, she said: "Tante Pelagie, I must tell you something, you and Tan'tante." She spoke low, but clearly and firmly. "I love you both,—please remember that I love you both. But I must go away from you. I can't live any longer here at Cote Joyeuse."

A spasm passed through Mam'selle Pauline's delicate frame. La Petite could feel the twitch of it in the wiry fingers that were intertwined with her own. Ma'ame Pelagie remained unchanged and motionless. No human eye could penetrate so deep as to see the satisfaction which her soul felt. She said: "What do you mean, Petite? Your father has sent you to us, and I am sure it is his wish that you remain."

"My father loves me, tante Pelagie, and such will not be his wish when he knows. Oh!" she continued with a restless, movement, "it is as though a weight were pressing me backward here. I must live another life; the life I lived before. I want to know things that are happening from day to day over the world, and hear them talked about. I want my music, my books, my companions. If I had known no other life but this one of privation, I suppose it would be different. If I had to live this life, I should make the best of it. But I do not have to; and you know, tante Pelagie, you do not need to. It seems to me," she added in a whisper, "that it is a sin against myself. Ah, Tan'tante!—what is the matter with Tan'tante?"

It was nothing; only a slight feeling of faintness, that would soon pass. She entreated them to take no notice; but they brought her some water and fanned her with a palmetto leaf.

But that night, in the stillness of the room, Mam'selle Pauline sobbed and would not be comforted. Ma'ame Pelagie took her in her arms.

"Pauline, my little sister Pauline," she entreated, "I never have seen you like this before. Do you no longer love me? Have we not been happy together, you and I?"

"Oh, yes, Sesoeur."

"Is it because La Petite is going away?"

"Yes, Sesoeur."

"Then she is dearer to you than I!" spoke Ma'ame Pelagie with sharp resentment. "Than I, who held you and warmed you in my arms the day you were born; than I, your mother, father, sister, everything that could cherish you. Pauline, don't tell me that."

Mam'selle Pauline tried to talk through her sobs.

"I can't explain it to you, Sesoeur. I don't understand it myself. I love you as I have always loved you; next to God. But if La Petite goes away I shall die. I can't understand,—help me, Sesoeur. She seems—she seems like a saviour; like one who had come and taken me by the hand and was leading me somewhere-somewhere I want to go."

Ma'ame Pelagie had been sitting beside the bed in her peignoir and slippers. She held the hand of her sister who lay there, and smoothed down the woman's soft brown hair. She said not a word, and the silence was broken only by Mam'selle Pauline's continued sobs. Once Ma'ame Pelagie arose to mix a drink of orange-flower water, which she gave to her sister, as she would have offered it to a nervous, fretful child. Almost an hour passed before Ma'ame Pelagie spoke again. Then she said:—

"Pauline, you must cease that sobbing, now, and sleep. You will make yourself ill. La Petite will not go away. Do you hear me? Do you understand? She will stay, I promise you."

Mam'selle Pauline could not clearly comprehend, but she had great faith in the word of her sister, and soothed by the promise and the touch of Ma'ame Pelagie's strong, gentle hand, she fell asleep.

III

Ma'ame Pelagie, when she saw that her sister slept, arose noiselessly and stepped outside upon the low-roofed narrow gallery. She did not linger there, but with a step that was hurried and agitated, she crossed the distance that divided her cabin from the ruin.

The night was not a dark one, for the sky was clear and the moon resplendent. But light or dark would have made no difference to Ma'ame Pelagie. It was not the first time she had stolen away to the ruin at night-time, when the whole plantation slept; but she never before had been there with a heart so nearly broken. She was going there for the last time to dream her dreams; to see the visions that hitherto had crowded her days and nights, and to bid them farewell.

There was the first of them, awaiting her upon the very portal; a robust old white-haired man, chiding her for returning home so late. There are guests to be entertained. Does she not know it? Guests from the city and from the near plantations. Yes, she knows it is late. She had been abroad with Felix, and they did not notice how the time was speeding. Felix is there; he will explain it all. He is there beside her, but she does not want to hear what he will tell her father.

Ma'ame Pelagie had sunk upon the bench where she and her sister so often came to sit. Turning, she gazed in through the gaping chasm of the window at her side. The interior of the ruin is ablaze. Not with the moonlight, for that is faint beside the other one—the sparkle from the crystal candelabra, which negroes, moving noiselessly and respectfully about, are lighting, one after the other. How the gleam of them reflects and glances from the polished marble pillars!

The room holds a number of guests. There is old Monsieur Lucien Santien, leaning against one of the pillars, and laughing at something which Monsieur Lafirme is telling him, till his fat shoulders shake. His son Jules is with him—Jules, who wants to marry her. She laughs. She wonders if Felix has told her father yet. There is young Jerome Lafirme playing at checkers upon the sofa with Leandre. Little Pauline stands annoying them and disturbing the game. Leandre reproves her. She begins to cry, and old black Clementine, her nurse, who is not far off, limps across the room to pick her up and carry her away. How sensitive the little one is! But she trots about and takes care of herself better than she did a year or two ago, when she fell upon the stone hall floor and raised a great "bo-bo" on her forehead. Pelagie was hurt and angry enough about it; and she ordered rugs and buffalo robes to be brought and laid thick upon the tiles, till the little one's steps were surer.

"Il ne faut pas faire mal a Pauline." She was saying it aloud—"faire mal a Pauline."

But she gazes beyond the salon, back into the big dining hall, where the white crepe myrtle grows. Ha! how low that bat has circled. It has struck Ma'ame Pelagie full on the breast. She does not know it. She is beyond there in the dining hall, where her father sits with a group of friends over their wine. As usual they are talking politics. How tiresome! She has heard them say "la guerre" oftener than once. La guerre. Bah! She and Felix have something pleasanter to talk about, out under the oaks, or back in the shadow of the oleanders.

But they were right! The sound of a cannon, shot at Sumter, has rolled across the Southern States, and its echo is heard along the whole stretch of Cote Joyeuse.

Yet Pelagie does not believe it. Not till La Ricaneuse stands before her with bare, black arms akimbo, uttering a volley of vile abuse and of brazen impudence. Pelagie wants to kill her. But yet she will not believe. Not till Felix comes to her in the chamber above the dining hall—there where that trumpet vine hangs—comes to say good-by to her. The hurt which the big brass buttons of his new gray uniform pressed into the tender flesh of her bosom has never left it. She sits upon the sofa, and he beside her, both speechless with pain. That room would not have been altered. Even the sofa would have been there in the same spot, and Ma'ame Pelagie had meant all along, for thirty years, all along, to lie there upon it some day when the time came to die.

But there is no time to weep, with the enemy at the door. The door has been no barrier. They are clattering through the halls now, drinking the wines, shattering the crystal and glass, slashing the portraits.

One of them stands before her and tells her to leave the house. She slaps his face. How the stigma stands out red as blood upon his blanched cheek!

Now there is a roar of fire and the flames are bearing down upon her motionless figure. She wants to show them how a daughter of Louisiana can perish before her conquerors. But little Pauline clings to her knees in an agony of terror. Little Pauline must be saved.

"Il ne faut pas faire mal a Pauline." Again she is saying it aloud—"faire mal a Pauline."

The night was nearly spent; Ma'ame Pelagie had glided from the bench upon which she had rested, and for hours lay prone upon the stone flagging, motionless. When she dragged herself to her feet it was to walk like one in a dream. About the great, solemn pillars, one after the other, she reached her arms, and pressed her cheek and her lips upon the senseless brick.

"Adieu, adieu!" whispered Ma'ame Pelagie.

There was no longer the moon to guide her steps across the familiar pathway to the cabin. The brightest light in the sky was Venus, that swung low in the east. The bats had ceased to beat their wings about the ruin. Even the mocking-bird that had warbled for hours in the old mulberry-tree had sung himself asleep. That darkest hour before the day was mantling the earth. Ma'ame Pelagie hurried through the wet, clinging grass, beating aside the heavy moss that swept across her face, walking on toward the cabin-toward Pauline. Not once did she look back upon the ruin that brooded like a huge monster—a black spot in the darkness that enveloped it.

IV

Little more than a year later the transformation which the old Valmet place had undergone was the talk and wonder of Cote Joyeuse. One would have looked in vain for the ruin; it was no longer there; neither was the log cabin. But out in the open, where the sun shone upon it, and the breezes blew about it, was a shapely structure fashioned from woods that the forests of the State had furnished. It rested upon a solid foundation of brick.

Upon a corner of the pleasant gallery sat Leandre smoking his afternoon cigar, and chatting with neighbors who had called. This was to be his pied a terre now; the home where his sisters and his daughter dwelt. The laughter of young people was heard out under the trees, and within the house where La Petite was playing upon the piano. With the enthusiasm of a young artist she drew from the keys strains that seemed marvelously beautiful to Mam'selle Pauline, who stood enraptured near her. Mam'selle Pauline had been touched by the re-creation of Valmet. Her cheek was as full and almost as flushed as La Petite's. The years were falling away from her.

Ma'ame Pelagie had been conversing with her brother and his friends. Then she turned and walked away; stopping to listen awhile to the music which La Petite was making. But it was only for a moment. She went on around the curve of the veranda, where she found herself alone. She stayed there, erect, holding to the banister rail and looking out calmly in the distance across the fields.

She was dressed in black, with the white kerchief she always wore folded across her bosom. Her thick, glossy hair rose like a silver diadem from her brow. In her deep, dark eyes smouldered the light of fires that would never flame. She had grown very old. Years instead of months seemed to have passed over her since the night she bade farewell to her visions.

Poor Ma'ame Pelagie! How could it be different! While the outward pressure of a young and joyous existence had forced her footsteps into the light, her soul had stayed in the shadow of the ruin.

DESIREE'S BABY

As the day was pleasant, Madame Valmonde drove over to L'Abri to see Desiree and the baby.

It made her laugh to think of Desiree with a baby. Why, it seemed but yesterday that Desiree was little more than a baby herself; when Monsieur in riding through the gateway of Valmonde had found her lying asleep in the shadow of the big stone pillar.

The little one awoke in his arms and began to cry for "Dada." That was as much as she could do or say. Some people thought she might have strayed there of her own accord, for she was of the toddling age. The prevailing belief was that she had been purposely left by a party of Texans, whose canvas-covered wagon, late in the day, had crossed the ferry that Coton Mais kept, just below the plantation. In time Madame Valmonde abandoned every speculation but the one that Desiree had been sent to her by a beneficent Providence to be the child of her affection, seeing that she was without child of the flesh. For the girl grew to be beautiful and gentle, affectionate and sincere,—the idol of Valmonde.

It was no wonder, when she stood one day against the stone pillar in whose shadow she had lain asleep, eighteen years before, that Armand Aubigny riding by and seeing her there, had fallen in love with her. That was the way all the Aubignys fell in love, as if struck by a pistol shot. The wonder was that he had not loved her before; for he had known her since his father brought him home from Paris, a boy of eight, after his mother died there. The passion that awoke in him that day, when he saw her at the gate, swept along like an avalanche, or like a prairie fire, or like anything that drives headlong over all obstacles.

Monsieur Valmonde grew practical and wanted things well considered: that is, the girl's obscure origin. Armand looked into her eyes and did not care. He was reminded that she was nameless. What did it matter about a name when he could give her one of the oldest and proudest in Louisiana? He ordered the corbeille from Paris, and contained himself with what patience he could until it arrived; then they were married.

Madame Valmonde had not seen Desiree and the baby for four weeks. When she reached L'Abri she shuddered at the first sight of it, as she always did. It was a sad looking place, which for many years had not known the gentle presence of a mistress, old Monsieur Aubigny having married and buried his wife in France, and she having loved her own land too well ever to leave it. The roof came down steep and black like a cowl, reaching out beyond the wide galleries that encircled the yellow stuccoed house. Big, solemn oaks grew close to it, and their thick-leaved, far-reaching branches shadowed it like a pall. Young Aubigny's rule was a strict one, too, and under it his negroes had forgotten how to be gay, as they had been during the old master's easy-going and indulgent lifetime.

The young mother was recovering slowly, and lay full length, in her soft white muslins and laces, upon a couch. The baby was beside her, upon her arm, where he had fallen asleep, at her breast. The yellow nurse woman sat beside a window fanning herself.

Madame Valmonde bent her portly figure over Desiree and kissed her, holding her an instant tenderly in her arms. Then she turned to the child.

"This is not the baby!" she exclaimed, in startled tones. French was the language spoken at Valmonde in those days.

"I knew you would be astonished," laughed Desiree, "at the way he has grown. The little cochon de lait! Look at his legs, mamma, and his hands and fingernails,—real finger-nails. Zandrine had to cut them this morning. Isn't it true, Zandrine?"

The woman bowed her turbaned head majestically, "Mais si, Madame."

"And the way he cries," went on Desiree, "is deafening. Armand heard him the other day as far away as La Blanche's cabin."

Madame Valmonde had never removed her eyes from the child. She lifted it and walked with it over to the window that was lightest. She scanned the baby narrowly, then looked as searchingly at Zandrine, whose face was turned to gaze across the fields.

"Yes, the child has grown, has changed," said Madame Valmonde, slowly, as she replaced it beside its mother. "What does Armand say?"

Desiree's face became suffused with a glow that was happiness itself.

"Oh, Armand is the proudest father in the parish, I believe, chiefly because it is a boy, to bear his name; though he says not,—that he would have loved a girl as well. But I know it isn't true. I know he says that to please me. And mamma," she added, drawing Madame Valmonde's head down to her, and speaking in a whisper, "he hasn't punished one of them—not one of them—since baby is born. Even Negrillon, who pretended to have burnt his leg that he might rest from work—he only laughed, and said Negrillon was a great scamp. Oh, mamma, I'm so happy; it frightens me."

What Desiree said was true. Marriage, and later the birth of his son had softened Armand Aubigny's imperious and exacting nature greatly. This was what made the gentle Desiree so happy, for she loved him desperately. When he frowned she trembled, but loved him. When he smiled, she asked no greater blessing of God. But Armand's dark, handsome face had not often been disfigured by frowns since the day he fell in love with her.

When the baby was about three months old, Desiree awoke one day to the conviction that there was something in the air menacing her peace. It was at first too subtle to grasp. It had only been a disquieting suggestion; an air of mystery among the blacks; unexpected visits from far-off neighbors who could hardly account for their coming. Then a strange, an awful change in her husband's manner, which she dared not ask him to explain. When he spoke to her, it was with averted eyes, from which the old love-light seemed to have gone out. He absented himself from home; and when there, avoided her presence and that of her child, without excuse. And the very spirit of Satan seemed suddenly to take hold of him in his dealings with the slaves. Desiree was miserable enough to die.

She sat in her room, one hot afternoon, in her peignoir, listlessly drawing through her fingers the strands of her long, silky brown hair that hung about her shoulders. The baby, half naked, lay asleep upon her own great mahogany bed, that was like a sumptuous throne, with its satin-lined half-canopy. One of La Blanche's little quadroon boys—half naked too—stood fanning the child slowly with a fan of peacock feathers. Desiree's eyes had been fixed absently and sadly upon the baby, while she was striving to penetrate the threatening mist that she felt closing about her. She looked from her child to the boy who stood beside him, and back again; over and over. "Ah!" It was a cry that she could not help; which she was not conscious of having uttered. The blood turned like ice in her veins, and a clammy moisture gathered upon her face.

She tried to speak to the little quadroon boy; but no sound would come, at first. When he heard his name uttered, he looked up, and his mistress was pointing to the door. He laid aside the great, soft fan, and obediently stole away, over the polished floor, on his bare tiptoes.

She stayed motionless, with gaze riveted upon her child, and her face the picture of fright.

Presently her husband entered the room, and without noticing her, went to a table and began to search among some papers which covered it.

"Armand," she called to him, in a voice which must have stabbed him, if he was human. But he did not notice. "Armand," she said again. Then she rose and tottered towards him. "Armand," she panted once more, clutching his arm, "look at our child. What does it mean? tell me."

He coldly but gently loosened her fingers from about his arm and thrust the hand away from him. "Tell me what it means!" she cried despairingly.

"It means," he answered lightly, "that the child is not white; it means that you are not white."

A quick conception of all that this accusation meant for her nerved her with unwonted courage to deny it. "It is a lie; it is not true, I am white! Look at my hair, it is brown; and my eyes are gray, Armand, you know they are gray. And my skin is fair," seizing his wrist. "Look at my hand; whiter than yours, Armand," she laughed hysterically.

"As white as La Blanche's," he returned cruelly; and went away leaving her alone with their child.

When she could hold a pen in her hand, she sent a despairing letter to Madame Valmonde.

"My mother, they tell me I am not white. Armand has told me I am not white. For God's sake tell them it is not true. You must know it is not true. I shall die. I must die. I cannot be so unhappy, and live."

The answer that came was brief:

"My own Desiree: Come home to Valmonde; back to your mother who loves you. Come with your child."

When the letter reached Desiree she went with it to her husband's study, and laid it open upon the desk before which he sat. She was like a stone image: silent, white, motionless after she placed it there.

In silence he ran his cold eyes over the written words.

He said nothing. "Shall I go, Armand?" she asked in tones sharp with agonized suspense.

"Yes, go."

"Do you want me to go?"

"Yes, I want you to go."

He thought Almighty God had dealt cruelly and unjustly with him; and felt, somehow, that he was paying Him back in kind when he stabbed thus into his wife's soul. Moreover he no longer loved her, because of the unconscious injury she had brought upon his home and his name.

She turned away like one stunned by a blow, and walked slowly towards the door, hoping he would call her back.

"Good-by, Armand," she moaned.

He did not answer her. That was his last blow at fate.

Desiree went in search of her child. Zandrine was pacing the sombre gallery with it. She took the little one from the nurse's arms with no word of explanation, and descending the steps, walked away, under the live-oak branches.

It was an October afternoon; the sun was just sinking. Out in the still fields the negroes were picking cotton.

Desiree had not changed the thin white garment nor the slippers which she wore. Her hair was uncovered and the sun's rays brought a golden gleam from its brown meshes. She did not take the broad, beaten road which led to the far-off plantation of Valmonde. She walked across a deserted field, where the stubble bruised her tender feet, so delicately shod, and tore her thin gown to shreds.

She disappeared among the reeds and willows that grew thick along the banks of the deep, sluggish bayou; and she did not come back again.

Some weeks later there was a curious scene enacted at L'Abri. In the centre of the smoothly swept back yard was a great bonfire. Armand Aubigny sat in the wide hallway that commanded a view of the spectacle; and it was he who dealt out to a half dozen negroes the material which kept this fire ablaze.

A graceful cradle of willow, with all its dainty furbishings, was laid upon the pyre, which had already been fed with the richness of a priceless layette. Then there were silk gowns, and velvet and satin ones added to these; laces, too, and embroideries; bonnets and gloves; for the corbeille had been of rare quality.

The last thing to go was a tiny bundle of letters; innocent little scribblings that Desiree had sent to him during the days of their espousal. There was the remnant of one back in the drawer from which he took them. But it was not Desiree's; it was part of an old letter from his mother to his father. He read it. She was thanking God for the blessing of her husband's love:—

"But above all," she wrote, "night and day, I thank the good God for having so arranged our lives that our dear Armand will never know that his mother, who adores him, belongs to the race that is cursed with the brand of slavery."

A RESPECTABLE WOMAN

Mrs. Baroda was a little provoked to learn that her husband expected his friend, Gouvernail, up to spend a week or two on the plantation.

They had entertained a good deal during the winter; much of the time had also been passed in New Orleans in various forms of mild dissipation. She was looking forward to a period of unbroken rest, now, and undisturbed tete-a-tete with her husband, when he informed her that Gouvernail was coming up to stay a week or two.

This was a man she had heard much of but never seen. He had been her husband's college friend; was now a journalist, and in no sense a society man or "a man about town," which were, perhaps, some of the reasons she had never met him. But she had unconsciously formed an image of him in her mind. She pictured him tall, slim, cynical; with eye-glasses, and his hands in his pockets; and she did not like him. Gouvernail was slim enough, but he wasn't very tall nor very cynical; neither did he wear eyeglasses nor carry his hands in his pockets. And she rather liked him when he first presented himself.

But why she liked him she could not explain satisfactorily to herself when she partly attempted to do so. She could discover in him none of those brilliant and promising traits which Gaston, her husband, had often assured her that he possessed. On the contrary, he sat rather mute and receptive before her chatty eagerness to make him feel at home and in face of Gaston's frank and wordy hospitality. His manner was as courteous toward her as the most exacting woman could require; but he made no direct appeal to her approval or even esteem.

Once settled at the plantation he seemed to like to sit upon the wide portico in the shade of one of the big Corinthian pillars, smoking his cigar lazily and listening attentively to Gaston's experience as a sugar planter.

"This is what I call living," he would utter with deep satisfaction, as the air that swept across the sugar field caressed him with its warm and scented velvety touch. It pleased him also to get on familiar terms with the big dogs that came about him, rubbing themselves sociably against his legs. He did not care to fish, and displayed no eagerness to go out and kill grosbecs when Gaston proposed doing so.

Gouvernail's personality puzzled Mrs. Baroda, but she liked him. Indeed, he was a lovable, inoffensive fellow. After a few days, when she could understand him no better than at first, she gave over being puzzled and remained piqued. In this mood she left her husband and her guest, for the most part, alone together. Then finding that Gouvernail took no manner of exception to her action, she imposed her society upon him, accompanying him in his idle strolls to the mill and walks along the batture. She persistently sought to penetrate the reserve in which he had unconsciously enveloped himself.

"When is he going—your friend?" she one day asked her husband. "For my part, he tires me frightfully."

"Not for a week yet, dear. I can't understand; he gives you no trouble."

"No. I should like him better if he did; if he were more like others, and I had to plan somewhat for his comfort and enjoyment."

Gaston took his wife's pretty face between his hands and looked tenderly and laughingly into her troubled eyes.

They were making a bit of toilet sociably together in Mrs. Baroda's dressing-room.

"You are full of surprises, ma belle," he said to her. "Even I can never count upon how you are going to act under given conditions." He kissed her and turned to fasten his cravat before the mirror.

"Here you are," he went on, "taking poor Gouvernail seriously and making a commotion over him, the last thing he would desire or expect."

"Commotion!" she hotly resented. "Nonsense! How can you say such a thing? Commotion, indeed! But, you know, you said he was clever."

"So he is. But the poor fellow is run down by overwork now. That's why I asked him here to take a rest."

"You used to say he was a man of ideas," she retorted, unconciliated. "I expected him to be interesting, at least. I'm going to the city in the morning to have my spring gowns fitted. Let me know when Mr. Gouvernail is gone; I shall be at my Aunt Octavie's."

That night she went and sat alone upon a bench that stood beneath a live oak tree at the edge of the gravel walk.

She had never known her thoughts or her intentions to be so confused. She could gather nothing from them but the feeling of a distinct necessity to quit her home in the morning.

Mrs. Baroda heard footsteps crunching the gravel; but could discern in the darkness only the approaching red point of a lighted cigar. She knew it was Gouvernail, for her husband did not smoke. She hoped to remain unnoticed, but her white gown revealed her to him. He threw away his cigar and seated himself upon the bench beside her; without a suspicion that she might object to his presence.

"Your husband told me to bring this to you, Mrs. Baroda," he said, handing her a filmy, white scarf with which she sometimes enveloped her head and shoulders. She accepted the scarf from him with a murmur of thanks, and let it lie in her lap.

He made some commonplace observation upon the baneful effect of the night air at the season. Then as his gaze reached out into the darkness, he murmured, half to himself:

"'Night of south winds—night of the large few stars! Still nodding night—'"

She made no reply to this apostrophe to the night, which, indeed, was not addressed to her.

Gouvernail was in no sense a diffident man, for he was not a self-conscious one. His periods of reserve were not constitutional, but the result of moods. Sitting there beside Mrs. Baroda, his silence melted for the time.

He talked freely and intimately in a low, hesitating drawl that was not unpleasant to hear. He talked of the old college days when he and Gaston had been a good deal to each other; of the days of keen and blind ambitions and large intentions. Now there was left with him, at least, a philosophic acquiescence to the existing order—only a desire to be permitted to exist, with now and then a little whiff of genuine life, such as he was breathing now.

Her mind only vaguely grasped what he was saying. Her physical being was for the moment predominant. She was not thinking of his words, only drinking in the tones of his voice. She wanted to reach out her hand in the darkness and touch him with the sensitive tips of her fingers upon the face or the lips. She wanted to draw close to him and whisper against his cheek—she did not care what—as she might have done if she had not been a respectable woman.

The stronger the impulse grew to bring herself near him, the further, in fact, did she draw away from him. As soon as she could do so without an appearance of too great rudeness, she rose and left him there alone.

Before she reached the house, Gouvernail had lighted a fresh cigar and ended his apostrophe to the night.

Mrs. Baroda was greatly tempted that night to tell her husband—who was also her friend—of this folly that had seized her. But she did not yield to the temptation. Beside being a respectable woman she was a very sensible one; and she knew there are some battles in life which a human being must fight alone.

When Gaston arose in the morning, his wife had already departed. She had taken an early morning train to the city. She did not return till Gouvernail was gone from under her roof.

There was some talk of having him back during the summer that followed. That is, Gaston greatly desired it; but this desire yielded to his wife's strenuous opposition.

However, before the year ended, she proposed, wholly from herself, to have Gouvernail visit them again. Her husband was surprised and delighted with the suggestion coming from her.

"I am glad, chere amie, to know that you have finally overcome your dislike for him; truly he did not deserve it."

"Oh," she told him, laughingly, after pressing a long, tender kiss upon his lips, "I have overcome everything! you will see. This time I shall be very nice to him."

THE KISS

It was still quite light out of doors, but inside with the curtains drawn and the smouldering fire sending out a dim, uncertain glow, the room was full of deep shadows.

Brantain sat in one of these shadows; it had overtaken him and he did not mind. The obscurity lent him courage to keep his eyes fastened as ardently as he liked upon the girl who sat in the firelight.

She was very handsome, with a certain fine, rich coloring that belongs to the healthy brune type. She was quite composed, as she idly stroked the satiny coat of the cat that lay curled in her lap, and she occasionally sent a slow glance into the shadow where her companion sat. They were talking low, of indifferent things which plainly were not the things that occupied their thoughts. She knew that he loved her—a frank, blustering fellow without guile enough to conceal his feelings, and no desire to do so. For two weeks past he had sought her society eagerly and persistently. She was confidently waiting for him to declare himself and she meant to accept him. The rather insignificant and unattractive Brantain was enormously rich; and she liked and required the entourage which wealth could give her.

During one of the pauses between their talk of the last tea and the next reception the door opened and a young man entered whom Brantain knew quite well. The girl turned her face toward him. A stride or two brought him to her side, and bending over her chair—before she could suspect his intention, for she did not realize that he had not seen her visitor—he pressed an ardent, lingering kiss upon her lips.

Brantain slowly arose; so did the girl arise, but quickly, and the newcomer stood between them, a little amusement and some defiance struggling with the confusion in his face.

"I believe," stammered Brantain, "I see that I have stayed too long. I—I had no idea—that is, I must wish you good-by." He was clutching his hat with both hands, and probably did not perceive that she was extending her hand to him, her presence of mind had not completely deserted her; but she could not have trusted herself to speak.

"Hang me if I saw him sitting there, Nattie! I know it's deuced awkward for you. But I hope you'll forgive me this once—this very first break. Why, what's the matter?"

"Don't touch me; don't come near me," she returned angrily. "What do you mean by entering the house without ringing?"

"I came in with your brother, as I often do," he answered coldly, in self-justification. "We came in the side way. He went upstairs and I came in here hoping to find you. The explanation is simple enough and ought to satisfy you that the misadventure was unavoidable. But do say that you forgive me, Nathalie," he entreated, softening.

"Forgive you! You don't know what you are talking about. Let me pass. It depends upon—a good deal whether I ever forgive you."

At that next reception which she and Brantain had been talking about she approached the young man with a delicious frankness of manner when she saw him there.

"Will you let me speak to you a moment or two, Mr. Brantain?" she asked with an engaging but perturbed smile. He seemed extremely unhappy; but when she took his arm and walked away with him, seeking a retired corner, a ray of hope mingled with the almost comical misery of his expression. She was apparently very outspoken.

"Perhaps I should not have sought this interview, Mr. Brantain; but—but, oh, I have been very uncomfortable, almost miserable since that little encounter the other afternoon. When I thought how you might have misinterpreted it, and believed things"—hope was plainly gaining the ascendancy over misery in Brantain's round, guileless face—"Of course, I know it is nothing to you, but for my own sake I do want you to understand that Mr. Harvy is an intimate friend of long standing. Why, we have always been like cousins—like brother and sister, I may say. He is my brother's most intimate associate and often fancies that he is entitled to the same privileges as the family. Oh, I know it is absurd, uncalled for, to tell you this; undignified even," she was almost weeping, "but it makes so much difference to me what you think of—of me." Her voice had grown very low and agitated. The misery had all disappeared from Brantain's face.

"Then you do really care what I think, Miss Nathalie? May I call you Miss Nathalie?" They turned into a long, dim corridor that was lined on either side with tall, graceful plants. They walked slowly to the very end of it. When they turned to retrace their steps Brantain's face was radiant and hers was triumphant.

Harvy was among the guests at the wedding; and he sought her out in a rare moment when she stood alone.

"Your husband," he said, smiling, "has sent me over to kiss you."

A quick blush suffused her face and round polished throat. "I suppose it's natural for a man to feel and act generously on an occasion of this kind. He tells me he doesn't want his marriage to interrupt wholly that pleasant intimacy which has existed between you and me. I don't know what you've been telling him," with an insolent smile, "but he has sent me here to kiss you."

She felt like a chess player who, by the clever handling of his pieces, sees the game taking the course intended. Her eyes were bright and tender with a smile as they glanced up into his; and her lips looked hungry for the kiss which they invited.

"But, you know," he went on quietly, "I didn't tell him so, it would have seemed ungrateful, but I can tell you. I've stopped kissing women; it's dangerous."

Well, she had Brantain and his million left. A person can't have everything in this world; and it was a little unreasonable of her to expect it.

A PAIR OF SILK STOCKINGS

Little Mrs. Sommers one day found herself the unexpected possessor of fifteen dollars. It seemed to her a very large amount of money, and the way in which it stuffed and bulged her worn old porte-monnaie gave her a feeling of importance such as she had not enjoyed for years.

The question of investment was one that occupied her greatly. For a day or two she walked about apparently in a dreamy state, but really absorbed in speculation and calculation. She did not wish to act hastily, to do anything she might afterward regret. But it was during the still hours of the night when she lay awake revolving plans in her mind that she seemed to see her way clearly toward a proper and judicious use of the money.

A dollar or two should be added to the price usually paid for Janie's shoes, which would insure their lasting an appreciable time longer than they usually did. She would buy so and so many yards of percale for new shirt waists for the boys and Janie and Mag. She had intended to make the old ones do by skilful patching. Mag should have another gown. She had seen some beautiful patterns, veritable bargains in the shop windows. And still there would be left enough for new stockings—two pairs apiece—and what darning that would save for a while! She would get caps for the boys and sailor-hats for the girls. The vision of her little brood looking fresh and dainty and new for once in their lives excited her and made her restless and wakeful with anticipation.

The neighbors sometimes talked of certain "better days" that little Mrs. Sommers had known before she had ever thought of being Mrs. Sommers. She herself indulged in no such morbid retrospection. She had no time—no second of time to devote to the past. The needs of the present absorbed her every faculty. A vision of the future like some dim, gaunt monster sometimes appalled her, but luckily to-morrow never comes.

Mrs. Sommers was one who knew the value of bargains; who could stand for hours making her way inch by inch toward the desired object that was selling below cost. She could elbow her way if need be; she had learned to clutch a piece of goods and hold it and stick to it with persistence and determination till her turn came to be served, no matter when it came.

But that day she was a little faint and tired. She had swallowed a light luncheon—no! when she came to think of it, between getting the children fed and the place righted, and preparing herself for the shopping bout, she had actually forgotten to eat any luncheon at all!

She sat herself upon a revolving stool before a counter that was comparatively deserted, trying to gather strength and courage to charge through an eager multitude that was besieging breastworks of shirting and figured lawn. An all-gone limp feeling had come over her and she rested her hand aimlessly upon the counter. She wore no gloves. By degrees she grew aware that her hand had encountered something very soothing, very pleasant to touch. She looked down to see that her hand lay upon a pile of silk stockings. A placard near by announced that they had been reduced in price from two dollars and fifty cents to one dollar and ninety-eight cents; and a young girl who stood behind the counter asked her if she wished to examine their line of silk hosiery. She smiled, just as if she had been asked to inspect a tiara of diamonds with the ultimate view of purchasing it. But she went on feeling the soft, sheeny luxurious things—with both hands now, holding them up to see them glisten, and to feel them glide serpent-like through her fingers.

Two hectic blotches came suddenly into her pale cheeks. She looked up at the girl.

"Do you think there are any eights-and-a-half among these?"

There were any number of eights-and-a-half. In fact, there were more of that size than any other. Here was a light-blue pair; there were some lavender, some all black and various shades of tan and gray. Mrs. Sommers selected a black pair and looked at them very long and closely. She pretended to be examining their texture, which the clerk assured her was excellent.

"A dollar and ninety-eight cents," she mused aloud. "Well, I'll take this pair." She handed the girl a five-dollar bill and waited for her change and for her parcel. What a very small parcel it was! It seemed lost in the depths of her shabby old shopping-bag.

Mrs. Sommers after that did not move in the direction of the bargain counter. She took the elevator, which carried her to an upper floor into the region of the ladies' waiting-rooms. Here, in a retired corner, she exchanged her cotton stockings for the new silk ones which she had just bought. She was not going through any acute mental process or reasoning with herself, nor was she striving to explain to her satisfaction the motive of her action. She was not thinking at all. She seemed for the time to be taking a rest from that laborious and fatiguing function and to have abandoned herself to some mechanical impulse that directed her actions and freed her of responsibility.

How good was the touch of the raw silk to her flesh! She felt like lying back in the cushioned chair and reveling for a while in the luxury of it. She did for a little while. Then she replaced her shoes, rolled the cotton stockings together and thrust them into her bag. After doing this she crossed straight over to the shoe department and took her seat to be fitted.

She was fastidious. The clerk could not make her out; he could not reconcile her shoes with her stockings, and she was not too easily pleased. She held back her skirts and turned her feet one way and her head another way as she glanced down at the polished, pointed-tipped boots. Her foot and ankle looked very pretty. She could not realize that they belonged to her and were a part of herself. She wanted an excellent and stylish fit, she told the young fellow who served her, and she did not mind the difference of a dollar or two more in the price so long as she got what she desired.

It was a long time since Mrs. Sommers had been fitted with gloves. On rare occasions when she had bought a pair they were always "bargains," so cheap that it would have been preposterous and unreasonable to have expected them to be fitted to the hand.

Now she rested her elbow on the cushion of the glove counter, and a pretty, pleasant young creature, delicate and deft of touch, drew a long-wristed "kid" over Mrs. Sommers's hand. She smoothed it down over the wrist and buttoned it neatly, and both lost themselves for a second or two in admiring contemplation of the little symmetrical gloved hand. But there were other places where money might be spent.

There were books and magazines piled up in the window of a stall a few paces down the street. Mrs. Sommers bought two high-priced magazines such as she had been accustomed to read in the days when she had been accustomed to other pleasant things. She carried them without wrapping. As well as she could she lifted her skirts at the crossings. Her stockings and boots and well fitting gloves had worked marvels in her bearing—had given her a feeling of assurance, a sense of belonging to the well-dressed multitude.

She was very hungry. Another time she would have stilled the cravings for food until reaching her own home, where she would have brewed herself a cup of tea and taken a snack of anything that was available. But the impulse that was guiding her would not suffer her to entertain any such thought.

There was a restaurant at the corner. She had never entered its doors; from the outside she had sometimes caught glimpses of spotless damask and shining crystal, and soft-stepping waiters serving people of fashion.

When she entered her appearance created no surprise, no consternation, as she had half feared it might. She seated herself at a small table alone, and an attentive waiter at once approached to take her order. She did not want a profusion; she craved a nice and tasty bite—a half dozen blue-points, a plump chop with cress, a something sweet—a creme-frappee, for instance; a glass of Rhine wine, and after all a small cup of black coffee.

While waiting to be served she removed her gloves very leisurely and laid them beside her. Then she picked up a magazine and glanced through it, cutting the pages with a blunt edge of her knife. It was all very agreeable. The damask was even more spotless than it had seemed through the window, and the crystal more sparkling. There were quiet ladies and gentlemen, who did not notice her, lunching at the small tables like her own. A soft, pleasing strain of music could be heard, and a gentle breeze, was blowing through the window. She tasted a bite, and she read a word or two, and she sipped the amber wine and wiggled her toes in the silk stockings. The price of it made no difference. She counted the money out to the waiter and left an extra coin on his tray, whereupon he bowed before her as before a princess of royal blood.

There was still money in her purse, and her next temptation presented itself in the shape of a matinee poster.

It was a little later when she entered the theatre, the play had begun and the house seemed to her to be packed. But there were vacant seats here and there, and into one of them she was ushered, between brilliantly dressed women who had gone there to kill time and eat candy and display their gaudy attire. There were many others who were there solely for the play and acting. It is safe to say there was no one present who bore quite the attitude which Mrs. Sommers did to her surroundings. She gathered in the whole—stage and players and people in one wide impression, and absorbed it and enjoyed it. She laughed at the comedy and wept—she and the gaudy woman next to her wept over the tragedy. And they talked a little together over it. And the gaudy woman wiped her eyes and sniffled on a tiny square of filmy, perfumed lace and passed little Mrs. Sommers her box of candy.

The play was over, the music ceased, the crowd filed out. It was like a dream ended. People scattered in all directions. Mrs. Sommers went to the corner and waited for the cable car.

A man with keen eyes, who sat opposite to her, seemed to like the study of her small, pale face. It puzzled him to decipher what he saw there. In truth, he saw nothing-unless he were wizard enough to detect a poignant wish, a powerful longing that the cable car would never stop anywhere, but go on and on with her forever.

THE LOCKET

I

One night in autumn a few men were gathered about a fire on the slope of a hill. They belonged to a small detachment of Confederate forces and were awaiting orders to march. Their gray uniforms were worn beyond the point of shabbiness. One of the men was heating something in a tin cup over the embers. Two were lying at full length a little distance away, while a fourth was trying to decipher a letter and had drawn close to the light. He had unfastened his collar and a good bit of his flannel shirt front.

"What's that you got around your neck, Ned?" asked one of the men lying in the obscurity.

Ned—or Edmond—mechanically fastened another button of his shirt and did not reply. He went on reading his letter.

"Is it your sweet heart's picture?"

"'Taint no gal's picture," offered the man at the fire. He had removed his tin cup and was engaged in stirring its grimy contents with a small stick. "That's a charm; some kind of hoodoo business that one o' them priests gave him to keep him out o' trouble. I know them Cath'lics. That's how come Frenchy got permoted an never got a scratch sence he's been in the ranks. Hey, French! aint I right?" Edmond looked up absently from his letter.

"What is it?" he asked.

"Aint that a charm you got round your neck?"

"It must be, Nick," returned Edmond with a smile. "I don't know how I could have gone through this year and a half without it."

The letter had made Edmond heart sick and home sick. He stretched himself on his back and looked straight up at the blinking stars. But he was not thinking of them nor of anything but a certain spring day when the bees were humming in the clematis; when a girl was saying good bye to him. He could see her as she unclasped from her neck the locket which she fastened about his own. It was an old fashioned golden locket bearing miniatures of her father and mother with their names and the date of their marriage. It was her most precious earthly possession. Edmond could feel again the folds of the girl's soft white gown, and see the droop of the angel-sleeves as she circled her fair arms about his neck. Her sweet face, appealing, pathetic, tormented by the pain of parting, appeared before him as vividly as life. He turned over, burying his face in his arm and there he lay, still and motionless.

The profound and treacherous night with its silence and semblance of peace settled upon the camp. He dreamed that the fair Octavie brought him a letter. He had no chair to offer her and was pained and embarrassed at the condition of his garments. He was ashamed of the poor food which comprised the dinner at which he begged her to join them.

He dreamt of a serpent coiling around his throat, and when he strove to grasp it the slimy thing glided away from his clutch. Then his dream was clamor.

"Git your duds! you! Frenchy!" Nick was bellowing in his face. There was what appeared to be a scramble and a rush rather than any regulated movement. The hill side was alive with clatter and motion; with sudden up-springing lights among the pines. In the east the dawn was unfolding out of the darkness. Its glimmer was yet dim in the plain below.

"What's it all about?" wondered a big black bird perched in the top of the tallest tree. He was an old solitary and a wise one, yet he was not wise enough to guess what it was all about. So all day long he kept blinking and wondering.

The noise reached far out over the plain and across the hills and awoke the little babes that were sleeping in their cradles. The smoke curled up toward the sun and shadowed the plain so that the stupid birds thought it was going to rain; but the wise one knew better.

"They are children playing a game," thought he. "I shall know more about it if I watch long enough."

At the approach of night they had all vanished away with their din and smoke. Then the old bird plumed his feathers. At last he had understood! With a flap of his great, black wings he shot downward, circling toward the plain.

A man was picking his way across the plain. He was dressed in the garb of a clergyman. His mission was to administer the consolations of religion to any of the prostrate figures in whom there might yet linger a spark of life. A negro accompanied him, bearing a bucket of water and a flask of wine.

There were no wounded here; they had been borne away. But the retreat had been hurried and the vultures and the good Samaritans would have to look to the dead.

There was a soldier—a mere boy—lying with his face to the sky. His hands were clutching the sward on either side and his finger nails were stuffed with earth and bits of grass that he had gathered in his despairing grasp upon life. His musket was gone; he was hatless and his face and clothing were begrimed. Around his neck hung a gold chain and locket. The priest, bending over him, unclasped the chain and removed it from the dead soldier's neck. He had grown used to the terrors of war and could face them unflinchingly; but its pathos, someway, always brought the tears to his old, dim eyes.

The angelus was ringing half a mile away. The priest and the negro knelt and murmured together the evening benediction and a prayer for the dead.

II

The peace and beauty of a spring day had descended upon the earth like a benediction. Along the leafy road which skirted a narrow, tortuous stream in central Louisiana, rumbled an old fashioned cabriolet, much the worse for hard and rough usage over country roads and lanes. The fat, black horses went in a slow, measured trot, notwithstanding constant urging on the part of the fat, black coachman. Within the vehicle were seated the fair Octavie and her old friend and neighbor, Judge Pillier, who had come to take her for a morning drive.

Octavie wore a plain black dress, severe in its simplicity. A narrow belt held it at the waist and the sleeves were gathered into close fitting wristbands. She had discarded her hoopskirt and appeared not unlike a nun. Beneath the folds of her bodice nestled the old locket. She never displayed it now. It had returned to her sanctified in her eyes; made precious as material things sometimes are by being forever identified with a significant moment of one's existence.

A hundred times she had read over the letter with which the locket had come back to her. No later than that morning she had again pored over it. As she sat beside the window, smoothing the letter out upon her knee, heavy and spiced odors stole in to her with the songs of birds and the humming of insects in the air.

She was so young and the world was so beautiful that there came over her a sense of unreality as she read again and again the priest's letter. He told of that autumn day drawing to its close, with the gold and the red fading out of the west, and the night gathering its shadows to cover the faces of the dead. Oh! She could not believe that one of those dead was her own! with visage uplifted to the gray sky in an agony of supplication. A spasm of resistance and rebellion seized and swept over her. Why was the spring here with its flowers and its seductive breath if he was dead! Why was she here! What further had she to do with life and the living!

Octavie had experienced many such moments of despair, but a blessed resignation had never failed to follow, and it fell then upon her like a mantle and enveloped her.

"I shall grow old and quiet and sad like poor Aunt Tavie," she murmured to herself as she folded the letter and replaced it in the secretary. Already she gave herself a little demure air like her Aunt Tavie. She walked with a slow glide in unconscious imitation of Mademoiselle Tavie whom some youthful affliction had robbed of earthly compensation while leaving her in possession of youth's illusions.

As she sat in the old cabriolet beside the father of her dead lover, again there came to Octavie the terrible sense of loss which had assailed her so often before. The soul of her youth clamored for its rights; for a share in the world's glory and exultation. She leaned back and drew her veil a little closer about her face. It was an old black veil of her Aunt Tavie's. A whiff of dust from the road had blown in and she wiped her cheeks and her eyes with her soft, white handkerchief, a homemade handkerchief, fabricated from one of her old fine muslin petticoats.

"Will you do me the favor, Octavie," requested the judge in the courteous tone which he never abandoned, "to remove that veil which you wear. It seems out of harmony, someway, with the beauty and promise of the day."

The young girl obediently yielded to her old companion's wish and unpinning the cumbersome, sombre drapery from her bonnet, folded it neatly and laid it upon the seat in front of her.

"Ah! that is better; far better!" he said in a tone expressing unbounded relief. "Never put it on again, dear." Octavie felt a little hurt; as if he wished to debar her from share and parcel in the burden of affliction which had been placed upon all of them. Again she drew forth the old muslin handkerchief.

They had left the big road and turned into a level plain which had formerly been an old meadow. There were clumps of thorn trees here and there, gorgeous in their spring radiance. Some cattle were grazing off in the distance in spots where the grass was tall and luscious. At the far end of the meadow was the towering lilac hedge, skirting the lane that led to Judge Pillier's house, and the scent of its heavy blossoms met them like a soft and tender embrace of welcome.

As they neared the house the old gentleman placed an arm around the girl's shoulders and turning her face up to him he said: "Do you not think that on a day like this, miracles might happen? When the whole earth is vibrant with life, does it not seem to you, Octavie, that heaven might for once relent and give us back our dead?" He spoke very low, advisedly, and impressively. In his voice was an old quaver which was not habitual and there was agitation in every line of his visage. She gazed at him with eyes that were full of supplication and a certain terror of joy.

They had been driving through the lane with the towering hedge on one side and the open meadow on the other. The horses had somewhat quickened their lazy pace. As they turned into the avenue leading to the house, a whole choir of feathered songsters fluted a sudden torrent of melodious greeting from their leafy hiding places.

Octavie felt as if she had passed into a stage of existence which was like a dream, more poignant and real than life. There was the old gray house with its sloping eaves. Amid the blur of green, and dimly, she saw familiar faces and heard voices as if they came from far across the fields, and Edmond was holding her. Her dead Edmond; her living Edmond, and she felt the beating of his heart against her and the agonizing rapture of his kisses striving to awake her. It was as if the spirit of life and the awakening spring had given back the soul to her youth and bade her rejoice.

It was many hours later that Octavie drew the locket from her bosom and looked at Edmond with a questioning appeal in her glance.

"It was the night before an engagement," he said. "In the hurry of the encounter, and the retreat next day, I never missed it till the fight was over. I thought of course I had lost it in the heat of the struggle, but it was stolen."

"Stolen," she shuddered, and thought of the dead soldier with his face uplifted to the sky in an agony of supplication.

Edmond said nothing; but he thought of his messmate; the one who had lain far back in the shadow; the one who had said nothing.

A REFLECTION

Some people are born with a vital and responsive energy. It not only enables them to keep abreast of the times; it qualifies them to furnish in their own personality a good bit of the motive power to the mad pace. They are fortunate beings. They do not need to apprehend the significance of things. They do not grow weary nor miss step, nor do they fall out of rank and sink by the wayside to be left contemplating the moving procession.

Ah! that moving procession that has left me by the road-side! Its fantastic colors are more brilliant and beautiful than the sun on the undulating waters. What matter if souls and bodies are failing beneath the feet of the ever-pressing multitude! It moves with the majestic rhythm of the spheres. Its discordant clashes sweep upward in one harmonious tone that blends with the music of other worlds—to complete God's orchestra.

It is greater than the stars—that moving procession of human energy; greater than the palpitating earth and the things growing thereon. Oh! I could weep at being left by the wayside; left with the grass and the clouds and a few dumb animals. True, I feel at home in the society of these symbols of life's immutability. In the procession I should feel the crushing feet, the clashing discords, the ruthless hands and stifling breath. I could not hear the rhythm of the march.

Salve! ye dumb hearts. Let us be still and wait by the roadside.

At the 'Cadian Ball

Bobinôt, that big, brown, good-natured Bobinôt, had no intention of going to the ball, even though he knew Calixta would be there. For what came of those balls but heartache, and a sickening disinclination for work the whole week through, till Saturday night came again and his tortures began afresh? Why could he not love Ozéina, who would marry him to-morrow; or Fronie, or any one of a dozen others, rather than that little Spanish vixen? Calixta's slender foot had never touched Cuban soil; but her mother's had, and the Spanish was in her blood all the same. For that reason the prairie people forgave her much that they would not have overlooked in their own daughters or sisters.

Her eyes, — Bobinôt thought of her eyes, and weakened, — the bluest, the drowsiest, most tantalizing that ever looked into a man's, he thought of her flaxen hair that kinked worse than a mulatto's close to her head; that broad, smiling mouth and tip-tilted nose, that full figure; that voice like a rich contralto song, with cadences in it that must have been taught by Satan, for there was no one else to teach her tricks on that 'Cadian prairie. Bobinôt thought of them all as he plowed his rows of cane.

There had even been a breath of scandal whispered about her a year ago, when she went to Assumption,— but why talk of it? No one did now. "C'est Espagnol, ça," most of them said with lenient shoulder-shrugs. "Bon chien tient de race," the old men mumbled over their pipes, stirred by recollections. Nothing was made of it, except that Fronie threw it up to Calixta when the two quarreled and fought on the church steps after mass one Sunday, about a lover. Calixta swore roundly in fine 'Cadian French and with true Spanish spirit, and slapped Fronie's face. Fronie had slapped her back; "Tiens, bocotte, va!" "Espèce de lionèse; prends ça, et ça!" till the curé himself was obliged to hasten and make peace between them. Bobinôt thought of it all, and would not go to the ball.

But in the afternoon, over at Friedheimer's store, where he was buying a trace-chain, he heard some one say that Alcée Laballière would be there. Then wild horses could not have kept him away. He knew how it would be—or rather he did not know how it would be—if the handsome young planter came over to the ball as he sometimes did. If Alcée happened to be in a serious mood, he might only go to the card-room and play a round or two; or he might stand out on the galleries talking crops and politics with the old people. But there was no telling. A drink or two could put the devil in his head,—that was what Bobinôt said to himself, as he wiped the sweat from his brow with his red bandanna; a gleam from Calixta's eyes, a flash of her ankle, a twirl of her skirts could do the same. Yes, Bobinôt would go to the ball.

That was the year Alcée Laballière put nine hundred acres in rice. It was putting a good deal of money into the ground, but the returns promised to be glorious. Old Madame Laballière, sailing about the spacious galleries in her white volante, figured it all out in her head. Clarisse, her goddaughter helped her a little, and together they built more air-castles than enough. Alcée worked like a mule that time; and if he did not kill himself, it was because his constitution was an iron one. It was an every-day affair for him to come in from the field well-nigh exhausted, and wet to the waist. He did not mind if there were visitors; he left them to his mother and Clarisse. There were often guests: young men and women who came up from the city, which was but a few hours away, to visit his beautiful kinswoman. She was worth going a good deal farther than that to see. Dainty as a lily; hardy as a sunflower; slim, tall, graceful, like one of the reeds that grew in the marsh. Cold and kind and cruel by turn, and everything that was aggravating to Alcée.

He would have liked to sweep the place of those visitors, often. Of the men, above all, with their ways and their manners; their swaying of fans like women, and dandling about hammocks. He could have pitched them over the levee into the river, if it hadn't meant murder. That was Alcée. But he must have been crazy the day he came in from the rice-field, and, toil-stained as he was, clasped Clarisse by the arms and panted a volley of hot, blistering love-words into her face. No man had ever spoken love to her like that.

"Monsieur!" she exclaimed, looking him full in the eyes, without a quiver. Alcée's hands dropped and his glance wavered before the chill of her calm, clear eyes.

"Par exemple!" she muttered disdainfully, as she turned from him, deftly adjusting the careful toilet that he had so brutally disarranged.

That happened a day or two before the cyclone came that cut into the rice like fine steel. It was an awful thing, coming so swiftly, without a moment's warning in which to light a holy candle or set a piece of blessed palm burning. Old madame wept openly and said her beads, just as her son Didier, the New Orleans one, would have done. If such a thing had happened to Alphonse, the Laballière planting cotton up in Natchitoches, he would have raved and stormed like a second cyclone, and made his surroundings unbearable for a day or two. But Alcée took the misfortune differently. He looked ill and gray after it, and said nothing. His speechlessness was frightful. Clarisse's heart melted with tenderness; but when she offered her soft, purring words of condolence, he accepted them with mute indifference. Then she and her nénaine wept afresh in each other's arms.

A night or two later, when Clarisse went to her window to kneel there in the moonlight and say her prayers before retiring, she saw that Bruce, Alcée's negro servant, had led his master's saddle-horse noiselessly along the edge of the sward that bordered the gravel-path, and stood holding him near by. Presently, she heard Alcée quit his room, which was beneath her own, and traverse the lower portico. As he emerged from the shadow and crossed the strip of moonlight, she perceived that he carried a pair of well-filled saddle-bags which he at once flung across the animal's back. He then lost no time in mounting, and after a brief exchange of words with Bruce, went cantering away, taking no precaution to avoid the noisy gravel as the negro had done.

Clarisse had never suspected that it might be Alcée's custom to sally forth from the plantation secretly, and at such an hour; for it was nearly midnight. And had it not been for the telltale saddle-bags, she would only have crept to bed, to wonder, to fret and dream unpleasant dreams. But her impatience and anxiety would not be held in check. Hastily unbolting the shutters of her door that opened upon the gallery, she stepped outside and called softly to the old negro.

"Gre't Peter! Miss Clarisse. I was n' sho it was a ghos' o' w'at, stan'in' up dah, plumb in de night, dataway."

He mounted halfway up the long, broad flight of stairs. She was standing at the top.

"Bruce, w'ere has Monsieur Alcée gone?" she asked.

"W'y, he gone 'bout he business, I reckin," replied Bruce, striving to be noncommittal at the outset.

"W'ere has Monsieur Alcée gone?" she reiterated, stamping her bare foot. "I won't stan' any nonsense or any lies; mine, Bruce."

"I don' ric'lic ez I eva tole you lie yit, Miss Clarisse. Mista Alcée, he all broke up, sho."

"W'ere - has - he gone? Ah, Sainte Vierge! faut de la patience! butor, va!"

"W'en I was in he room, a-breshin' off he clo'es to-day," the darkey began, settling himself against the stair-rail, "he look dat speechless an' down, I say, 'You 'pear tu me like some pussun w'at gwine have a spell o' sickness, Mista Alcée.' He say, 'You reckin?' 'I dat he git up, go look hisse'f stiddy in de glass. Den he go to de chimbly an' jerk up de quinine bottle an po' a gre't hoss-dose on to he han'. An' he swalla dat mess in a wink, an' wash hit down wid a big dram o' w'iskey w'at he keep in he room, aginst he come all soppin' wet outen de fiel'.

"He 'lows, 'No, I ain' gwine be sick, Bruce.' Den he square off. He say, 'I kin mak out to stan' up an' gi' an' take wid any man I knows, lessen hit 's John L. Sulvun. But w'en God A'mighty an' a 'omen jines fo'ces agin me, dat 's one too many fur me.' I tell 'im, 'Jis so,' while' I 'se makin' out to bresh a spot off w'at ain' dah, on he coat colla. I tell 'im, 'You wants li'le res', suh.' He say, 'No, I wants li'le fling; dat w'at I wants; an I gwine git it. Pitch me a fis'ful o' clo'es in dem 'ar saddle-bags.' Dat w'at he say. Don't you bodda, missy. He jis' gone a-caperin' yonda to de Cajun ball. Uh - uh - de skeeters is fair' a-swarmin' like bees roun' yo' foots!"

The mosquitoes were indeed attacking Clarisse's white feet savagely. She had unconsciously been alternately rubbing one foot over the other during the darkey's recital.

"The 'Cadian ball," she repeated contemptously. "Humph! Par exemple! Nice conduc' for a Laballière. An' he needs a saddle-bag, fill' with clothes, to go to the 'Cadian ball!"

"Oh, Miss Clarisse; you go on to bed, chile; git yo' soun' sleep. He 'low he come back in couple weeks o' so. I kiarn be repeatin' lot o' truck w'at young mans say, out heah face o' a young gal."

Clarisse said no more, but turned and abruptly reentered the house.

"You done talk too much wid yo' mouf already, you ole fool nigga, you," muttered Bruce to himself as he walked away.

Alcée reached the ball very late, of course—too late for the chicken gumbo which had been served at midnight.

The big, low-ceiled room—they called it a hall—was packed with men and women dancing to the music of three fiddles. There were broad galleries all around it. There was a room at one side where sober-faced men were playing cards. Another, in which babies were sleeping, was called le parc aux petits. Any one who is white may go to a 'Cadian ball, but he must pay for his lemonade, his coffee and chicken gumbo. And he must behave himself like a 'Cadian. Grosboeuf was giving this ball. He had been giving them since he was a young man, and he was a middle-aged one, now. In that time he could recall but one disturbance, and that was caused by American railroaders, who were not in touch with their surroundings and had no business there. "Ces maudits gens du raiderode," Grosboeuf called them.

Alcée Laballière's presence at the ball caused a flutter even among the men, who could not but admire his "nerve" after such misfortune befalling him. To be sure, they knew the Laballières were rich—that there were resources East, and more again in the city. But they felt it took a brave homme to stand a blow like that philosophically. One old gentleman, who was in the habit of reading a Paris newspaper and knew things, chuckled gleefully to everybody that Alcée's conduct was altogether chic, mais chic. That he had more panache than Boulanger. Well, perhaps he had.

But what he did not show outwardly was that he was in a mood for ugly things to-night. Poor Bobinôt alone felt it vaguely. He discerned a gleam of it in Alcée's handsome eyes, as the young planter stood in the doorway, looking with rather feverish glance upon the assembly, while he laughed and talked with a 'Cadian farmer who was beside him.

Bobinôt himself was dull-looking and clumsy. Most of the men were. But the young women were very beautiful. The eyes that glanced into Alcée's as they passed him were big, dark, soft as those of the young heifers standing out in the cool prairie grass.

But the belle was Calixta. Her white dress was not nearly so handsome or well made as Fronie's (she and Fronie had quite forgotten the battle on the church steps, and were friends again), nor were her slippers so stylish as those of Ozéina; and she fanned herself with a handkerchief, since she had broken her red fan at the last ball, and her aunts and uncles were not willing to give her another. But all the men agreed she was at her best to-night. Such animation! and abandon! such flashes of wit!

"Hé, Bobinôt! Mais w'at's the matta? W'at you standin' planté là like ole Ma'ame Tina's cow in the bog, you?"

That was good. That was an excellent thrust at Bobinôt, who had forgotten the figure of the dance with his mind bent on other things, and it started a clamor of laughter at his expense. He joined good-naturedly. It was better to receive even such notice as that from Calixta than none at all. But Madame Suzonne, sitting in a corner, whispered to her neighbor that if Ozéina were to conduct herself in a like manner, she should immediately be taken out to the mule-cart and driven home. The women did not always approve of Calixta.

Now and then were short lulls in the dance, when couples flocked out upon the galleries for a brief respite and fresh air. The moon had gone down pale in the west, and in the east was yet no promise of day. After such an interval, when the dancers again assembled to resume the interrupted quadrille, Calixta was not among them.

She was sitting upon a bench out in the shadow, with Alcée beside her. They were acting like fools. He had attempted to take a little gold ring from her finger; just for the fun of it, for there was nothing he could have done with the ring but replace it again. But she clinched her hand tight. He pretended that it was a very difficult matter to open it. Then he kept the hand in his. They seemed to forget about it. He played with her ear-ring, a thin crescent of gold hanging from her small brown ear. He caught a wisp of the kinky hair that had escaped its fastening, and rubbed the ends of it against his shaven cheek.

"You know, last year in Assumption, Calixta?" They belonged to the younger generation, so preferred to speak English.

"Don't come say Assumption to me, M'sieur Alcée. I done yeard Assumption till I'm plumb sick."

"Yes, I know. The idiots! Because you were in Assumption, and I happened to go to Assumption, they must have it that we went together. But it was nice— hein, Calixta?—in Assumption?"

They saw Bobinôt emerge from the hall and stand a moment outside the lighted doorway, peering uneasily and searchingly into the darkness. He did not see them, and went slowly back.

"There is Bobinôt looking for you. You are going to set poor Bobinôt crazy. You'll marry him some day; hein, Calixta?"

"I don't say no, me," she replied, striving to withdraw her hand, which he held more firmly for the attempt.

"But come, Calixta; you know you said you would go back to Assumption, just to spite them."

"No, I neva said that, me. You mus' dreamt that."

"Oh, I thought you did. You know I 'm going down to the city."

"W'en?"

"To-night."

"Betta make has'e, then; it 's mos' day."

"Well, to-morrow 'll do."

"W'at you goin' do, yonda?"

"I don't know. Drown myself in the lake, maybe; unless you go down there to visit your uncle."

Calixta's senses were reeling; and they well-nigh left her when she felt Alcée's lips brush her ear like the touch of a rose.

"Mista Alcée! Is dat Mista Alcée?" the thick voice of a negro was asking; he stood on the ground, holding to the banister-rails near which the couple sat.

"W'at do you want now?" cried Alcée impatiently. "Can't I have a moment of peace?"

"I ben huntin' you high an' low, suh," answered the man. "Dey - dey some one in de road, onda de mulbare-tree, want see you a minute."

"I would n't go out to the road to see the Angel Gabriel. And if you come back here with any more talk, I 'll have to break your neck." The negro turned mumbling away.

Alcée and Calixta laughed softly about it. Her boisterousness was all gone. They talked low, and laughed softly, as lovers do.

"Alcée! Alcée Laballière!"

It was not the negro's voice this time; but one that went through Alcée's body like an electric shock, bringing him to his feet.

Clarisse was standing there in her riding-habit, where the negro had stood. For an instant confusion reigned in Alcée's thoughts, as with one who awakes suddenly from a dream. But he felt that something of serious import had brought his cousin to the ball in the dead of night.

"W'at does this mean, Clarisse?" he asked.

"It means something has happen' at home. You mus' come."

"Happened to maman?" he questioned, in alarm.

"No; nénaine is well, and asleep. It is something else. Not to frighten you. But you mus' come. Come with me, Alcée."

There was no need for the imploring note. He would have followed the voice anywhere.

She had now recognized the girl sitting back on the bench.

"Ah, c'est vous, Calixta? Comment ça va, mon enfant?"

"Tcha va b'en; et vous, mam'zélle?"

Alcée swung himself over the low rail and started to follow Clarisse, without a word, without a glance back at the girl. He had forgotten he was leaving her there. But Clarisse whispered something to him, and he turned back to say "Good-night, Calixta," and offer his hand to press through the railing. She pretended not to see it.

"How come that? You settin' yere by yo'se'f, Calixta?" It was Bobinôt who had found her there alone. The dancers had not yet come out. She looked ghastly in the faint, gray light struggling out of the east.

"Yes, that's me. Go yonda in the parc aux petits an' ask Aunt Olisse fu' my hat. She knows w'ere 't is. I want to go home, me."

"How you came?"

"I come afoot, with the Cateaus. But I 'm goin' now. I ent goin' wait fu' 'em. I 'm plumb wo' out, me."

"Kin I go with you, Calixta?"

"I don' care."

They went together across the open prairie and along the edge of the fields, stumbling in the uncertain light. He told her to lift her dress that was getting wet and bedraggled; for she was pulling at the weeds and grasses with her hands.

"I don' care; it 's got to go in the tub, anyway. You been sayin' all along you want to marry me, Bobinôt. Well, if you want, yet, I don' care, me."

The glow of a sudden and overwhelming happiness shone out in the brown, rugged face of the young Acadian. He could not speak, for very joy. It choked him.

"Oh well, if you don' want," snapped Calixta, flippantly, pretending to be piqued at his silence.

"Bon Dieu! You know that makes me crazy, w'at you sayin'. You mean that, Calixta? You ent goin' turn roun' agin?"

"I neva tole you that much yet, Bobinôt. I mean that. Tiens," and she held out her hand in the business-like manner of a man who clinches a bargain with a hand-clasp. Bobinôt grew bold with happiness and asked Calixta to kiss him. She turned her face, that was almost ugly after the night's dissipation, and looked steadily into his.

"I don' want to kiss you, Bobinôt," she said, turning away again, "not to-day. Some other time. Bonté divine! ent you satisfy, yet!"

"Oh, I 'm satisfy, Calixta," he said.

Riding through a patch of wood, Clarisse's saddle became ungirted, and she and Alcée dismounted to readjust it.

For the twentieth time he asked her what had happened at home.

"But, Clarisse, w'at is it? Is it a misfortune?"

"Ah Dieu sait!" It 's only something that happen' to me."

"To you!"

"I saw you go away las night, Alcée, with those saddle-bags," she said, haltingly, striving to arrange something about the saddle, "an' I made Bruce tell me. He said you had gone to the ball, an' wouldn' be home for weeks an' weeks. I thought, Alcée—maybe you were going to—to Assumption. I got wild. An' then I knew if you didn't come back, now, to-night, I could n't stan' it,—again."

She had her face hidden in her arm that she was resting against the saddle when she said that.

He began to wonder if this meant love. But she had to tell him so, before he believed it. And when she told him, he thought the face of the Universe was changed—just like Bobinôt. Was it last week the cyclone had well-nigh ruined him? The cyclone seemed a huge joke, now. It was he, then, who, an hour ago was kissing little Calixta's ear and whispering nonsense into it. Calixta was like a myth, now. The one, only, great reality in the world was Clarisse standing before him, telling him that she loved him.

In the distance they heard the rapid discharge of pistol-shots; but it did not disturb them. They knew it was only the negro musicians who had gone into the yard to fire their pistols into the air, as the custom is, and to announce "le bal est fini."

The Storm

I

The leaves were so still that even Bibi thought it was going to rain. Bobinôt, who was accustomed to converse on terms of perfect equality with his little son, called the child's attention to certain sombre clouds that were rolling with sinister intention from the west, accompanied by a sullen, threatening roar. They were at Friedheimer's store and decided to remain there till the storm had passed. They sat within the door on two empty kegs. Bibi was four years old and looked very wise.

"Mama'll be 'fraid, yes, he suggested with blinking eyes.

"She'll shut the house. Maybe she got Sylvie helpin' her this evenin'," Bobinôt responded reassuringly.

"No; she ent got Sylvie. Sylvie was helpin' her yistiday,' piped Bibi.

Bobinôt arose and going across to the counter purchased a can of shrimps, of which Calixta was very fond. Then he returned to his perch on the keg and sat stolidly holding the can of shrimps while the storm burst. It shook the wooden store and seemed to be ripping great furrows in the distant field. Bibi laid his little hand on his father's knee and was not afraid.

II

Calixta, at home, felt no uneasiness for their safety. She sat at a side window sewing furiously on a sewing machine. She was greatly occupied and did not notice the approaching storm. But she felt very warm and often stopped to mop her face on which the perspiration gathered in beads. She unfastened her white sacque at the throat. It began to grow dark, and suddenly realizing the situation she got up hurriedly and went about closing windows and doors.

Out on the small front gallery she had hung Bobinôt's Sunday clothes to dry and she hastened out to gather them before the rain fell. As she stepped outside, Alcée Laballière rode in at the gate. She had not seen him very often since her marriage, and never alone. She stood there with Bobinôt's coat in her hands, and the big rain drops began to fall. Alcée rode his horse under the shelter of a side projection where the chickens had huddled and there were plows and a harrow piled up in the corner.

"May I come and wait on your gallery till the storm is over, Calixta?" he asked.

Come 'long in, M'sieur Alcée."

His voice and her own startled her as if from a trance, and she seized Bobinôt's vest. Alcée, mounting to the porch, grabbed the trousers and snatched Bibi's braided jacket that was about to be carried away by a sudden gust of wind. He expressed an intention to remain outside, but it was soon apparent that he might as well have been out in the open: the water beat in upon the boards in driving sheets, and he went inside, closing the door after him. It was even necessary to put something beneath the door to keep the water out.

"My! what a rain! It's good two years sence it rain' like that," exclaimed Calixta as she rolled up a piece of bagging and Alcée helped her to thrust it beneath the crack.

She was a little fuller of figure than five years before when she married; but she had lost nothing of her vivacity. Her blue eyes still retained their melting quality; and her yellow hair, dishevelled by the wind and rain, kinked more stubbornly than ever about her ears and temples.

The rain beat upon the low, shingled roof with a force and clatter that threatened to break an entrance and deluge them there. They were in the dining room—the sitting room—the general utility room. Adjoining was her bed room, with Bibi's couch along side her own. The door stood open, and the room with its white, monumental bed, its closed shutters, looked dim and mysterious.

Alcée flung himself into a rocker and Calixta nervously began to gather up from the floor the lengths of a cotton sheet which she had been sewing.

If this keeps up, Dieu sait if the levees goin' to stan it!" she exclaimed.

"What have you got to do with the levees?"

"I got enough to do! An' there's Bobinôt with Bibi out in that storm—if he only didn' left Friedheimer's!"

"Let us hope, Calixta, that Bobinôt's got sense enough to come in out of a cyclone."

She went and stood at the window with a greatly disturbed look on her face. She wiped the frame that was clouded with moisture. It was stiflingly hot. Alcée got up and joined her at the window, looking over her shoulder. The rain was coming down in sheets obscuring the view of far-off cabins and enveloping the distant wood in a gray mist. The playing of the lightning was incessant. A bolt struck a tall chinaberry tree at the edge of the field. It filled all visible space with a blinding glare and the crash seemed to invade the very boards they stood upon.

Calixta put her hands to her eyes, and with a cry, staggered backward. Alcée's arm encircled her, and for an instant he drew her close and spasmodically to him.

"Bonté!" she cried, releasing herself from his encircling arm and retreating from the window, the house'll go next! If I only knew w'ere Bibi was!" She would not compose herself; she would not be seated. Alcée clasped her shoulders and looked into her face. The contact of her warm, palpitating body when he had unthinkingly drawn her into his arms, had aroused all the old-time infatuation and desire for her flesh.

"Calixta," he said, "don't be frightened. Nothing can happen. The house is too low to be struck, with so many tall trees standing about. There! aren't you going to be quiet? say, aren't you?" He pushed her hair back from her face that was warm and steaming. Her lips were as red and moist as pomegranate seed. Her white neck and a glimpse of her full, firm bosom disturbed him powerfully. As she glanced up at him the fear in her liquid blue eyes had given place to a drowsy gleam that unconsciously betrayed a sensuous desire. He looked down into her eyes and there was nothing for him to do but to gather her lips in a kiss. It reminded him of Assumption.

"Do you remember—in Assumption, Calixta?" he asked in a low voice broken by passion. Oh! she remembered; for in Assumption he had kissed her and kissed and kissed her; until his senses would well nigh fail, and to save her he would resort to a desperate flight. If she was not an immaculate dove in those days, she was still inviolate; a passionate creature whose very defenselessness had made her defense, against which his honor forbade him to prevail. Now—well, now—her lips seemed in a manner free to be tasted, as well as her round, white throat and her whiter breasts.

They did not heed the crashing torrents, and the roar of the elements made her laugh as she lay in his arms. She was a revelation in that dim, mysterious chamber; as white as the couch she lay upon. Her firm, elastic flesh that was knowing for the first time its birthright, was like a creamy lily that the sun invites to contribute its breath and perfume to the undying life of the world.

The generous abundance of her passion, without guile or trickery, was like a white flame which penetrated and found response in depths of his own sensuous nature that had never yet been reached.

When he touched her breasts they gave themselves up in quivering ecstasy, inviting his lips. Her mouth was a fountain of delight. And when he possessed her, they seemed to swoon together at the very borderland of life's mystery.

He stayed cushioned upon her, breathless, dazed, enervated, with his heart beating like a hammer upon her. With one hand she clasped his head, her lips lightly touching his forehead. The other hand stroked with a soothing rhythm his muscular shoulders.

The growl of the thunder was distant and passing away. The rain beat softly upon the shingles, inviting them to drowsiness and sleep. But they dared not yield.

III

The rain was over; and the sun was turning the glistening green world into a palace of gems. Calixta, on the gallery, watched Alcée ride away. He turned and smiled at her with a beaming face; and she lifted her pretty chin in the air and laughed aloud.

Bobinôt and Bibi, trudging home, stopped without at the cistern to make themselves presentable.

"My! Bibi, w'at will yo' mama say! You ought to be ashame'. You oughta' put on those good pants. Look at 'em! An' that mud on yo' collar! How you got that mud on yo' collar, Bibi? I never saw such a boy!" Bibi was the picture of pathetic resignation. Bobinôt was the embodiment of serious solicitude as he strove to remove from his own person and his son's the signs of their tramp over heavy roads and through wet fields. He scraped the mud off Bibi's bare legs and feet with a stick and carefully removed all traces from his heavy brogans. Then, prepared for the worst—the meeting with an over-scrupulous housewife, they entered cautiously at the back door.

Calixta was preparing supper. She had set the table and was dripping coffee at the hearth. She sprang up as they came in.

"Oh, Bobinôt! You back! My! but I was uneasy. W'ere you been during the rain? An' Bibi? he ain't wet? he ain't hurt?" She had clasped Bibi and was kissing him effusively. Bobinôt's explanations and apologies which he had been composing all along the way, died on his lips as Calixta felt him to see if he were dry, and seemed to express nothing but satisfaction at their safe return.

"I brought you some shrimps, Calixta," offered Bobinôt, hauling the can from his ample side pocket and laying it on the table.

"Shrimps! Oh, Bobinôt! you too good fo' anything!" and she gave him a smacking kiss on the cheek that resounded, "J'vous réponds, we'll have a feas' to-night! umph-umph!"

Bobinôt and Bibi began to relax and enjoy themselves, and when the three seated themselves at table they laughed much and so loud that anyone might have heard them as far away as Laballière's.

IV

Alcée Laballière wrote to his wife, Clarisse, that night. It was a loving letter, full of tender solicitude. He told her not to hurry back, but if she and the babies liked it at Biloxi, to stay a month longer. He was getting on nicely; and though he missed them, he was willing to bear the separation a while longer—realizing that their health and pleasure were the first things to be considered.

V

As for Clarisse, she was charmed upon receiving her husband's letter. She and the babies were doing well. The society was agreeable; many of her old friends and acquaintances were at the bay. And the first free breath since her marriage seemed to restore the pleasant liberty of her maiden days. Devoted as she was to her husband, their intimate conjugal life was something which she was more than willing to forego for a while.

So the storm passed and every one was happy.

The Story of an Hour

Knowing that Mrs. Mallard was afflicted with a heart trouble, great care was taken to break to her as gently as possible the news of her husband's death.

It was her sister Josephine who told her, in broken sentences; veiled hints that revealed in half concealing. Her husband's friend Richards was there, too, near her. It was he who had been in the newspaper office when intelligence of the railroad disaster was received, with Brently Mallard's name leading the list of "killed." He had only taken the time to assure himself of its truth by a second telegram, and had hastened to forestall any less careful, less tender friend in bearing the sad message.

She did not hear the story as many women have heard the same, with a paralyzed inability to accept its significance. She wept at once, with sudden, wild abandonment, in her sister's arms. When the storm of grief had spent itself she went away to her room alone. She would have no one follow her.

There stood, facing the open window, a comfortable, roomy armchair. Into this she sank, pressed down by a physical exhaustion that haunted her body and seemed to reach into her soul.

She could see in the open square before her house the tops of trees that were all aquiver with the new spring life. The delicious breath of rain was in the air. In the street below a peddler was crying his wares. The notes of a distant song which some one was singing reached her faintly, and countless sparrows were twittering in the eaves.

There were patches of blue sky showing here and there through the clouds that had met and piled one above the other in the west facing her window.

She sat with her head thrown back upon the cushion of the chair, quite motionless, except when a sob came up into her throat and shook her, as a child who has cried itself to sleep continues to sob in its dreams.

She was young, with a fair, calm face, whose lines bespoke repression and even a certain strength. But now there was a dull stare in her eyes, whose gaze was fixed away off yonder on one of those patches of blue sky. It was not a glance of reflection, but rather indicated a suspension of intelligent thought.

There was something coming to her and she was waiting for it, fearfully. What was it? She did not know; it was too subtle and elusive to name. But she felt it, creeping out of the sky, reaching toward her through the sounds, the scents, the color that filled the air.

Now her bosom rose and fell tumultuously. She was beginning to recognize this thing that was approaching to possess her, and she was striving to beat it back with her will--as powerless as her two white slender hands would have been. When she abandoned herself a little whispered word escaped her slightly parted lips. She said it over and over under hte breath: "free, free, free!" The vacant stare and the look of terror that had followed it went from her eyes. They stayed keen and bright. Her pulses beat fast, and the coursing blood warmed and relaxed every inch of her body.

She did not stop to ask if it were or were not a monstrous joy that held her. A clear and exalted perception enabled her to dismiss the suggestion as trivial. She knew that she would weep again when she saw the kind, tender hands folded in death; the face that had never looked save with love upon her, fixed and gray and dead. But she saw beyond that bitter moment a long procession of years to come that would belong to her absolutely. And she opened and spread her arms out to them in welcome.

There would be no one to live for during those coming years; she would live for herself. There would be no powerful will bending hers in that blind persistence with which men and women believe they have a right to impose a private will upon a fellow-creature. A kind intention or a cruel intention made the act seem no less a crime as she looked upon it in that brief moment of illumination.

And yet she had loved him--sometimes. Often she had not. What did it matter! What could love, the unsolved mystery, count for in the face of this possession of self-assertion which she suddenly recognized as the strongest impulse of her being!

"Free! Body and soul free!" she kept whispering.

Josephine was kneeling before the closed door with her lips to the keyhold, imploring for admission. "Louise, open the door! I beg; open the door--you will make yourself ill. What are you doing, Louise? For heaven's sake open the door."

"Go away. I am not making myself ill." No; she was drinking in a very elixir of life through that open window.

Her fancy was running riot along those days ahead of her. Spring days, and summer days, and all sorts of days that would be her own. She breathed a quick prayer that life might be long. It was only yesterday she had thought with a shudder that life might be long.

She arose at length and opened the door to her sister's importunities. There was a feverish triumph in her eyes, and she carried herself unwittingly like a goddess of Victory. She clasped her sister's waist, and together they descended the stairs. Richards stood waiting for them at the bottom.

Some one was opening the front door with a latchkey. It was Brently Mallard who entered, a little travel-stained, composedly carrying his grip-sack and umbrella. He had been far from the scene of the accident, and did not even know there had been one. He stood amazed at Josephine's piercing cry; at Richards' quick motion to screen him from the view of his wife.

When the doctors came they said she had died of heart disease--of the joy that kills.

Printed in Great Britain
by Amazon

41454067R00030